for my parents

Library of Congress Cataloging-in-Publication Data
Cooper, Elisha.
Farm / by Elisha Cooper. — 1st ed.
p. cm.
Summary: Describes the activities on a busy family farm from the spring when preparations for planting begin to the autumn when the cats grow winter coats and the cold rains begin to fall.
ISBN 978-0-545-07075-1
[1. Farm life — Fiction. 2. Farms — Fiction.] I. Title.
PZ7.C784737Far 2010
[E] — dc22
2009004342

10 9 8 7 6 5 4 3 2 1   10 11 12 13 14
First edition, April 2010
Printed in Singapore 46

The text type was set in Rockwell.
Watercolor and pencil were used for the paintings in this book.
Book design by Polly Kanevsky

GLOSSARY

ALFALFA: A leafy green plant that is used as feed for farm animals

AUGER: A screw-shaped machine that shoots grain and corn through a tube

CHAFF: Dusty bits of seed and cuttings left over after a harvest

COMBINE HARVESTER: A big harvesting machine that combines two operations, like cutting and threshing

FERTILIZER: A substance added to the soil to make it more fertile, increasing the yield of the harvest

GRAIN ELEVATOR: A large building with a mechanical elevator inside that is used for storing grain

HUSK: The leafy outer cover of the corncob

KERNELS: The seeds of the corn

PESTICIDE: A chemical that kills insects that would ruin a particular crop

PIT: The hole in the ground where corn is dropped

SILO: A round tower used for storing crops

THRESHER: A machine that separates kernels from a cob, or grain from a stem

TILLER: A machine that turns soil over and prepares the land for growing crops

YIELD: The quantity or amount of a crop that is produced

FARM

ELISHA COOPER

Orchard Books | New York | An Imprint of Scholastic Inc.

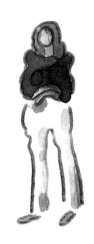

Take a farmer, another farmer, a boy, a girl.

Add a house,

two barns,

four silos,

some sheds,

three tractors,

some trucks,

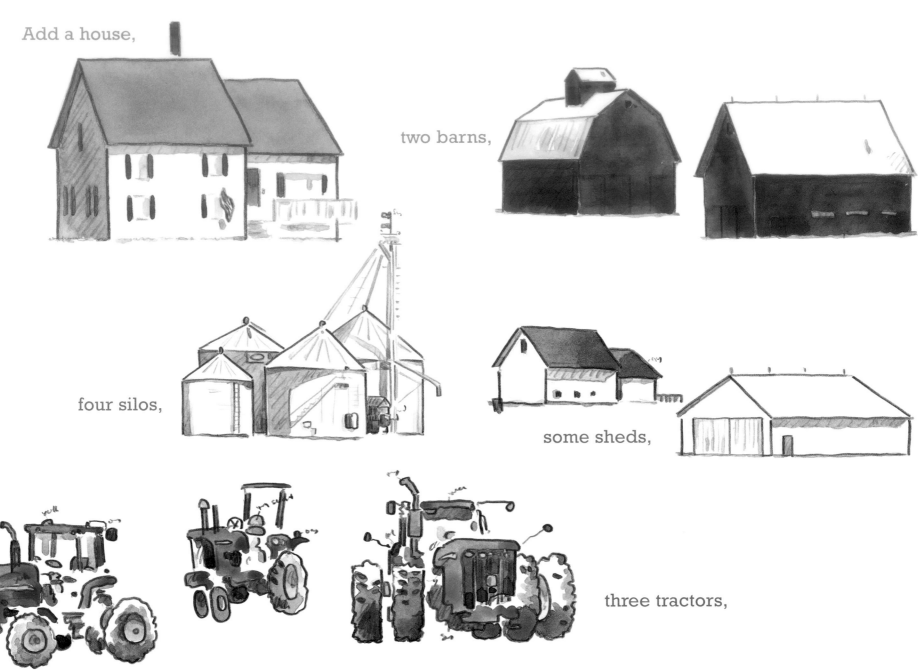
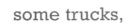

a few farmhands,

and plenty of equipment.

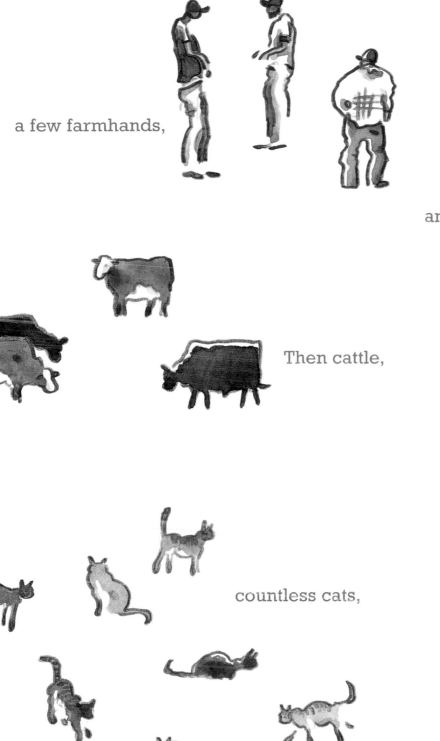

Then cattle,

chickens,

countless cats,

a dog.

Put them all together and you get . . .

. . . a farm.

Fields lie underneath the farm. The fields are flat,
stretching as far as the eye can see. There are no hills.

Clouds race overhead, almost touching the fields below.
Early in the spring, the fields are bare dirt. A tractor rumbles back and forth.

Inside the tractor, the farmer drinks coffee and listens to weather reports on the radio.
Every once in a while, he turns in his seat to check the tiller.

The tiller turns the soil, preparing it for planting. Dirt pops into the air, and
the fields change from the color of milk chocolate to the color of dark chocolate.

The tractor stops. The farmer stares at the engine. He calls a neighbor on his cell phone, the neighbor brings a new part, and together they fix the tractor.

It starts to rain. The tractor stops again. March is a mud month and weather must be dry for tilling. The farmer will have to wait. Weather can't be fixed

In April, the mornings grow lighter.
Before school, the girl feeds the cattle, and the boy feeds the chickens.
Morning chores would be better if they didn't happen every morning.

After school, the girl and boy plant tomato, carrot,
and green bean seeds in the garden. They plant
sweet corn — the kind that people eat.
Some chores don't seem like chores.

The farmer plants feed corn — the kind that animals eat.
The tractor pulls a planter that drops seeds into the soil in
long straight rows. The planter looks like a big green beetle.

The days warm. The barn doors stay open. The barn smells of hay and
manure and engine grease. It smells of dust. Dust covers everything:
shovels and buckets, swallow nests and spiderwebs, a toy tractor,
a chair with three legs, the handprints of the girl and boy in the concrete floor.

Even the barn cats are dusty.

Some of the barn cats don't have names.
Some do. There's Oreo. She's black and white.
She's sweet, and good at catching mice.

There's Claw. He's always scratching
something — the dog, the other cats, the barn.

Fern has a purr bigger than she is,
   and a tail she wraps around the legs
      of anyone who walks past.

Martha S. is constantly cleaning
herself with her tongue. She's
very clean, for a barn cat.

The dog is named Homer.
Homer stays outside most of the time.
His job is to guard the farm.

Bear won't let anyone touch her. She just
had kittens and hides them in the hayloft.
Cats can look after themselves.

Homer and Fern are friends. She sheds when
   she leans on him. Together they walk around
      the barnyard and keep things in order.

Homer spends the rest of the day waiting for
the farmer to come in from the fields. Sometimes,
when he is bored, he bounces the chickens.

The chickens scurry around the barnyard, avoiding Homer. The roosters strut behind the hens, looking important.

One rooster is named Breakfast.
The other is named Biggie.
The hens don't have names.

The cattle don't have names, either. They have number tags in their ears, sandpaper tongues, and dark eyes with long lashes.

When the animals are not eating
or sleeping or grooming,
they are deep in thought.

Or so it seems.

Breakfast and Biggie
tilt their heads and
look curious.

Claw studies the barn wall.

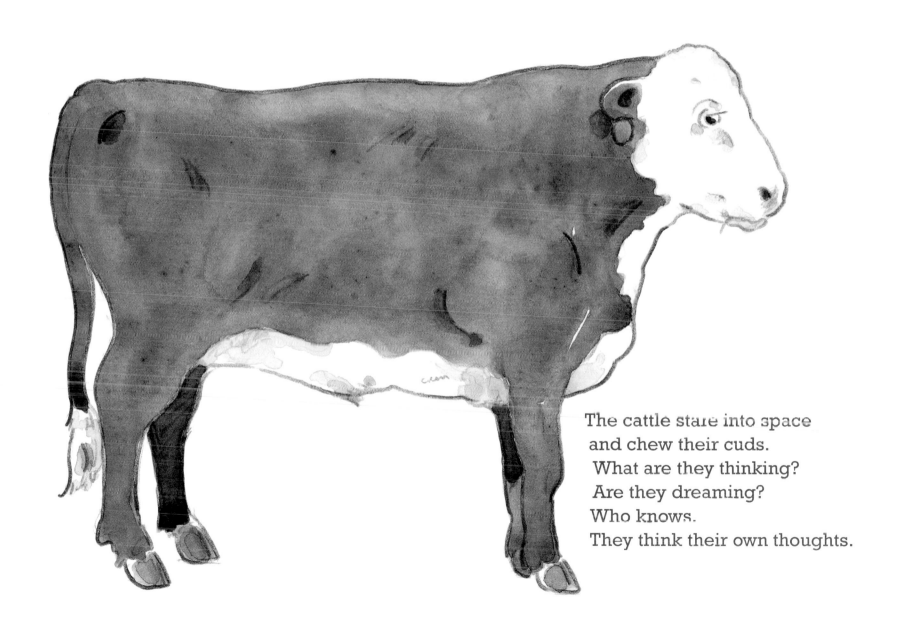

The cattle stare into space
and chew their cuds.
What are they thinking?
Are they dreaming?
Who knows.
They think their own thoughts.

Everything grows in May. The corn shoots up, high as the girl's knee. The rows look like wet hair just after it's combed. The farmer combs the rows with the tractor, spraying fertilizer and pesticide. Then the rows grow together and the fields become an ocean of green. The farms are like islands on the ocean. The tractors are like boats.

At the edge of the fields, butterflies bounce. In the garden, bees zoom from bud to bud.

The girl steps on a bee. The boy gets bit by mosquitoes.
The cats swallow grasshoppers and hack them up. At night, everyone itches.

The land heats up and the farm is rich with smells.
The smell changes depending on which way the wind is blowing.

To the west is a hog farm.
No one likes it when the wind is from that direction.

To the north is a farm with fields of alfalfa.
Cut hay smells like summer.

To the east is a farm that
put up a cell phone tower.
It doesn't smell of anything.

To the south are more cornfields, which
smell sort of buttery. Beyond them is the town.

The work of planting is done. Things slow down. The farmer drives into town to get a spare part for the tractor. School is out, so the girl and boy come, too. They stop for hamburgers. They stop for milk shakes.

On the way home, the farmer pulls over and talks to
a neighbor about crop prices and vacation plans.

Out the open window, a water sprinkler
says *think-think-think*. June is a sweet month.

Other animals enjoy June, too.

Breakfast takes a dust bath.

Homer steals green beans from the garden.

The cattle mosey around and poop:

plip, plap, plop.

Claw scratches himself.

Bear plays with a snake then eats it (some animals enjoy June more than others).

At dusk, wild animals come out.

Skunks shuffle across the lawn.

Rabbits nibble through the garden.

Chipmunks skitter over the road (they make it most of the time).

Pheasants stalk among the corn.

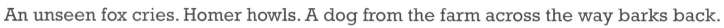
An unseen fox cries. Homer howls. A dog from the farm across the way barks back.

On the farm, even when it's dark, some animal is always awake.

The days grow humid. The cattle lie down.
They know first: thunderhead clouds
gathering at one end of the land.

The temperature drops. Birds dart for cover, the farmer
rushes to get things inside. A drop, another. *Whoosh*.

Sheets of water sweep the farm, hammering roofs and rattling windows. And then it is over. The corn all bends in one direction as if to say, *The storm went that way.*

After a storm, the farm swells with sound. The corn rustles. The cattle bellow.
A tractor echoes in and out. Birds quarrel. Bugs hum. Their hum is constant.

Even the clouds seem to make sound as they bump across the sky.
For a quiet place, the farm is not so quiet.

July is for exploring. The girl wanders to the creek with Homer and tries to catch catfish.

The boy tries to play with the cats, but they're not interested. So he heads to a neighbor's farm.
Other people's places are always more exciting.

The farmer drives the boy and girl into town, where they sell sweet corn from the back of the truck.

The girl picks more corn for dinner. She collects eggs. When she shucks the ears of corn, they squeak.

The boy picks tomatoes, carrots, beans. He throws tomatoes at birds until the farmer tells him to stop.

A delivery truck stops. Claw climbs inside before the boy shoos him out.
The truck brought an ice-cream maker. July is a good month for eating.

August is the hottest month. It's so steamy the horizon
shimmers. Everyone goes looking for shade.
The boy heads to the hayloft and builds forts
in the bales where he can hide.

Homer slinks to the barn
and lies on the cool concrete.
The cats are nowhere to be found.
The chickens have disappeared, too.

The cattle huddle under trees down by the creek. They swat flies off one another's noses with their tails.

The girl reads on the swing, until the sun finds her under the tree.

She heads into the fields, discovering shade under a roof of corn.

With summer's end, cooler weather comes to the farm. The evenings grow short. The corn rises above the farmer's head. The farms are disappearing under a rising ocean of corn.

The boy and girl start school. New classes, new friends.
One morning, the farmer tells them one of the roosters is missing.
Did a fox get it? September shows that some things are not forever.

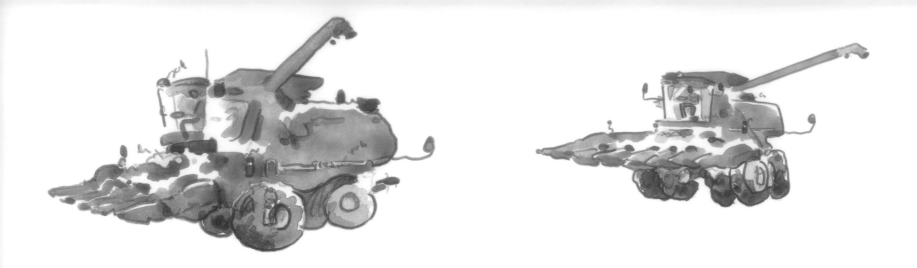

October is harvest time. The combine harvester is big as a barn, loud as a factory.
It roars through the field, gobbling up eight rows of corn at a time.

It bites stalks, pulls them into its mouth, separates kernel from cob in the thresher inside its belly,
burps out husks. Once full, the combine spits a stream of corn into waiting wagons and trucks.

Sometimes, to save time, the combine fills the wagons as they
drive through the field. Birds whirl behind in the chaff, eating insects.

The farmer checks the corn's yield on his computer,
talks with other farmers on his cell phone, and eats a sandwich.

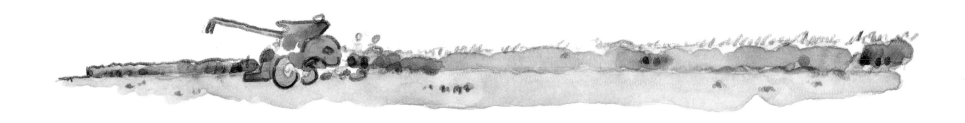

Wagons and trucks drive to the silos and dump corn into the pit.
The corn shoots through the auger into the silo. Kernels rattle against
the silo's metal sides like someone typing very loud and very fast. The silos fill up.

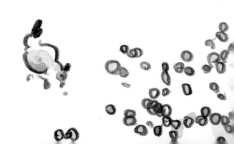

Corn is everywhere. Drifting across the silos,
spilling out of the wagons, and scattering around
the barnyard. The boy helps the farmer shovel it up.

After drying for a month, the corn will be hauled to the
town's grain elevators, loaded on railcars and barges, and
sent all over the world to feed cattle and be made into food.

November breaks clear and cold. The cats grow winter coats. The chickens
stay indoors. The cattle are sent to market. In the barn, the farmer drinks coffee
and works on a tractor. The girl is not around as much, thinking about other things.
Homer sits on the porch, waiting for her to come home.

Leaves scatter over the farm. The fields are dirt again, ready for
next year. In the evening, geese fly over the fields. An autumn rain falls,
and as the seasons of the farm turn, the water seeps into the earth.